E $7.99
Sa   Savitz, Harriet
           The pail of
nails

DATE DUE

MR 15 '89			
JE 16 '89			
SE 21 '93			
MAY 31 96			
NOV 10 97			
AG 30 '99			
MR 06 '01			
AG 12 '79			

DEMCO

The Pail of Nails

By Harriet May Savitz
and K. Michael Syring

Illustrated by
Sister Jane Mary Sorosiak, O.S.F.

Ottawa Hills Press   4525 Brookside Road   Ottawa Hills, Ohio 43615

Marcus had sad eyes and a face that didn't smile much. He lived by the Sea of Galilee. He didn't have a father. His father had been a soldier in a forgotten war. He had never returned from that war.

Marcus walked on the sand by the Sea of Galilee. He walked alone. He thought of many things.

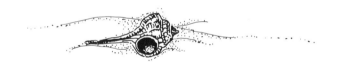

He thought of war.

He thought of his father
whom he would
never see again.

He thought of his mother who cried a lot at night. Marcus knew why she cried. But he couldn't help her.

While he sat on the beach by the sea, Marcus liked to watch the fishermen work on their nets before they went fishing for the day. Marcus wanted to be a fisherman. He wanted a boat of his own. He wanted his own nets. He wanted to bring his own prizes back from the sea.

But Marcus knew he couldn't have everything he wanted.
He wanted his father. He couldn't have him back.

One day a man walked down the beach. He walked toward Marcus and smiled. The man's smile made Marcus want to smile back, and he did. Marcus thought the man must be a fisherman, for he seemed to be such a good friend to the fishermen whose boats disappeared daily at sea. Sometimes, early in the morning, the man would join his fishermen friends at sea.

"Is it a good fishing day?" Marcus asked finally, his shyness leaving him.

The man sat down next to him. "No," he shook his head, "but it is a good day anyway."

They became good friends that day.
They talked about fishing. Marcus liked that.
He didn't have a father to talk to about
things like fishing. They talked about boats.
Marcus liked that too. And his new friend
told stories. He told stories about people
loving one another. It filled Marcus with a
warm feeling. He wished he had a story to tell.

The fisherman was a gentle man. He told Marcus he had never been to war. He told Marcus that his father had told him that war was bad. Marcus understood. He didn't like killing either. Most boys of his age took pride in wrestling, in fighting, in being the strongest of the strong. Marcus wasn't like them.

They met many times after that. They met when the sky was dark with clouds and rain threatened the Sea of Galilee. Marcus' new friend spoke of peace. They met when the wind whipped the sand and mixed it with the sea. The man said to Marcus, "Some day, you will have your boat, if you really work for it, and if you keep love in your heart."

This man had many friends. They talked, ran and laughed together on the beach. Marcus laughed too. They played ball together. Marcus didn't feel alone anymore.

One day Marcus went to the beach as usual, but as soon as he stepped on the sand, he knew something was wrong. There were no boats on the Sea of Galilee. He looked as far up and down the beach as he could see. None of his friends were there. And his best friend, the fisherman, was gone too. A wave of loneliness fell upon Marcus.

He went back to the beach the next day and the next. Still the beach was empty. There was no one to laugh with. There was no one to play ball with. Marcus wondered where his friend had gone. Why had he left without saying goodbye?

Marcus didn't know it, but he was leaving too.

The next day his mother received a message. It came from Marcus' uncle in Jerusalem. There was trouble in the land. Small wars were breaking out everywhere.

"Come stay with me for awhile," the uncle wrote, "Be safe."

Marcus' mother said yes.

Marcus said goodbye to the Sea of
Galilee. He felt now, surely, he would never
again see his friend, the fisherman.

He and his mother traveled to Jerusalem. It took about five days. They passed the town of Cana. Marcus remembered his friend had said he went there once. Could he be there now? The desert air was hot. Marcus missed the breezes of the Sea of Galilee.

Jerusalem was a big city, the biggest Marcus had ever seen. From a distance, the buildings looked like towers of gold. The streets were filled with soldiers and excitement was everywhere. It was Passover, the Jewish holiday. Even the Governor was there. People were coming to Jerusalem from everywhere.

Marcus and his mother settled at his
uncle's house. And then his uncle said,
"Come, let us go and watch the festivities."

They went to the center of the city.
Marcus had never seen so many people
gathered in one place before. He was
surprised when a soldier marching in the
parade grabbed him by the hand and pulled
him into the marching line. His uncle
seemed pleased. His mother didn't have a
chance to say anything.

And then the soldier beside him said, "Here boy,
carry this pail of large nails for me.
I have carried it long enough."

How proud Marcus was to be the youngest boy in the parade. Suddenly he felt very much part of the celebration. He forgot that he didn't like war, that he didn't like killing. He even forgot the words of the fisherman, the words about peace and love. Instead, came a feeling of pride. He felt strong and brave. Many of the people in the crowds jeered as he and the soldiers walked by. But carrying the pail of nails, walking with so many strong men around him, Marcus wasn't afraid.

So Marcus, along with the pail of nails, found himself in his first parade, laughing with many of the soldiers, walking along proudly, with his mother and uncle watching and waving.

They walked through the town, then out of Jerusalem.
Suddenly the parade stopped. Soon Marcus heard someone call out,
"Where is the boy with the pail of nails?"

Marcus stepped forward, feeling very proud. He walked past the soldiers to the head of the parade. His father would have been so proud of him today. And then he was there in front of the long line of soldiers, in front of all the people who had run in the streets along the sides of the parade. He held the pail of nails, but he could not speak. Marcus just stood there, his eyes open wide, not believing what he saw in front of him.

There, lying on the ground, was his fisherman friend, who looked at him with understanding in his eyes. Someone took the pail of nails from Marcus. Someone took his fisherman friend and nailed him to the cross.

Marcus looked around. Why didn't someone help his friend? Why didn't someone speak up? Where were all the friends who had run and laughed on the beach? Were they too afraid to help him now? Was this a part of war? Why were the soldiers happy? What could his fisherman friend have done so wrong?

He looked into the crowd of faces for his mother and uncle.

He could not see them.

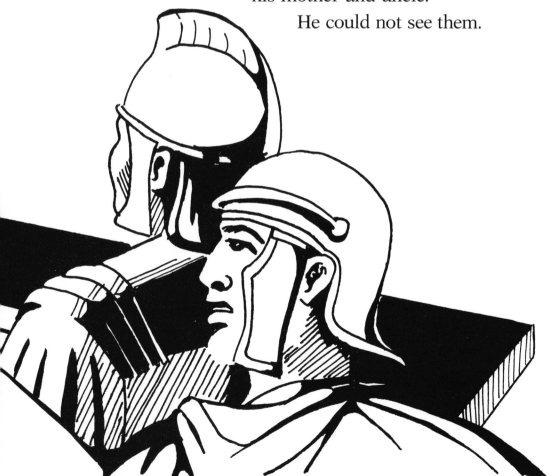

So Marcus stood there in front of his friend on the cross, feeling the pain that his friend felt. He looked up at him, wanting to ask, "Why? How? What for?" But his friend looked down and shook his head as if to say, "Don't speak."

Marcus just stood there in silence with the empty pail of nails at his feet. The people behind him began to leave. The sun slid slowly down behind the cross. His uncle said, "Come, Marcus, it's time to go." But Marcus shook his head and explained that he must stay with his friend for a little while longer.

His uncle waited down the road. Marcus felt his mother's worried eyes as he stood there, under the cross. His friend couldn't talk anymore. He wouldn't be able to tell anybody that war was bad, that love was good, and that all men were brothers. But then, why had his brothers nailed him to the cross?

The sky grew dark, but still Marcus stood there. And as he stood there, he grew less lonely, and less lonely, until he didn't feel lonely at all. He felt as if the empty spot inside him had been filled.

His mother came at last to get him. "Marcus," she asked as they walked away from the cross, "How did you know that man?"

Marcus didn't answer. The answers were deep in his heart. But as he walked down the road, away from the cross, he knew what he would do.

Some day he would go back to the Sea of Galilee. Some day he would have his own boat, his own nets, his own prize from the sea. He would work toward that dream as his friend had told him to.

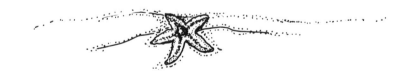

And wherever he went, he would remember the fisherman and tell his stories of love . . . and peace. That way his friend would always be with him, and he would never be alone again.

The End

Harriet May Savitz

Ask Harriet May Savitz why she's a writer and she'll probably tell you that she doesn't really know. "I just don't know why I do it . . . except that the creative process holds the greatest amount of joy when it all comes together."

Harriet Savitz' previous books have been about the physically disabled, about people of courage, about fighters, about people who love and feel and hate and who are different only in the fact that they sit, not stand, through life. Books by Harriet May Savitz include *Fly, Wheels, Fly, The Lionhearted, On The Move, Wheelchair Champions,* and *Run, Don't Walk.*

Mrs. Savitz has lectured at East Tennessee State University, Villanova University, Mansfield State College, and was a speaker at the Mid-Atlantic Library Conference. In addition, Mrs. Savitz teaches writing at the Philadelphia Writers' Conference, holds workshops in novel writing, and has been guest lecturer of English Literature at the University of Pennsylvania.

K. Michael Syring

Michael Syring is a Toledo businessman who had a story, an idea, which he felt needed to be told. A children's story, a simple story about friendship and faith.

The story stayed with him for many years. Sometimes, when he had the need, he would repeat it to interested listeners.

One day, he told the story to Harriet May Savitz. She joined with him in feeling that it should be shared with others and offered her writing talent to make it a reality. Together, they wrote the book, *The Pail of Nails.*

Sister Jane Mary Sorosiak, O.S.F.

Sister Jane Mary devoted her entire life to art, to the teaching of art and to her religious calling in the order of the Sisters of St. Francis.

Presently, she is teaching art at Lourdes College, Sylvania, Ohio. She also utilizes her art talent to execute cover designs for various civic and church publications, does murals, provides watercolor, oil and acrylic paintings, does calligraphy for groups and individuals, and illustrates lecture and demonstration visuals and displays.